Alessandra Benassi

THE SEA, A SAIL

...

A DREAM

Youcanprint *Self-Publishing*

Title | The sea, a sail...a dream
Author | Alessandra Benassi

ISBN | 978-88-93212-76-2

Youcanprint Self-Publishing
Via Roma, 73 – 73039 Tricase (LE) – Italy
www.youcanprint.it
info@youcanprint.it
Facebook: facebook.com/youcanprint.it
Twitter: twitter.com/youcanprintit

FOREWORD

Two years ago I chose to take a break in a place I hadn't been to for a while. I had childhood memories of that place. Vivid, wonderful memories. And so I had a very strong desire to go back and see if it had changed. I was surprised - very much so. A last-minute decision had taken me back to a place I didn't remember loving so much. And that very week something happened. Something unexpected. I was sitting under a pine tree one later summer afternoon, down by the beach. The sun had gone in and grey clouds had taken over. It was raining and windy, and the beach was deserted, but I stayed there under that pine tree. I was writing. I've always loved rough seas and solitude. The lure of the wind and the tides. It helps me to think, write, and feel good. Then suddenly, I remember, my gaze wandered, because it encountered that man, who instead of retreating, was going out to meet the sea. And in him I saw the same love I have always felt for the waves.

He was wearing a wetsuit and carried a board and a sail. What happened next was incredible, and I'll never forget it. And even now, with the distance of time, that loving look has stayed in my heart, just as my love for the sea has always been there, in my heart.

Always and forever...

LIFE

I
who live on unlimited passion
unconfined love
and devotion to a sport.
I
who like anyone else
live on hopes,
dreams
and uncertainties.
Every day I risk,
pushing my limits
and my fears
in the search for that perfection
that will perhaps
never come.
I
who have the sense of control
and think positive always.
I set myself goals
and the constant drive to achieve them
every day that passes,
makes me a better person.
I
who know how to listen
because my mind and my body

are one and the same.
And now
I'm here,
before the start
and I focus my attention on myself.
I visualise every sensation I feel
and every thought
that touches my mind.
I follow my body's movement
in my mind
and memorise it.
I memorise the perfect sequence.
Yes.
I close my eyes a moment
and listen.
I hear only the beating of my heart.
It's time.
We're off.
I open my eyes.
Go.

MY WORLD

I am here,
now,
in the middle of the sea.
I'm here
between one wave and the next
with my board
and the swell of the waves.
Suspended
in emptiness
in a reality all my own,
I live my world
with the sun in my eyes
and the sea wind
warming my back.
As if in a dream
I reach out
and touch the sky with a fingertip.
And then I leap.
I turn the sail
and leap again.
I leap beyond the sea,
beyond the wind,
beyond borders.
The border of the old world
and the threshold of the new.

And as if suspended
in infinite time
I'm now
in this new world
that belongs to few.
In a fantasy
that many dream of.

MY LOVE FOR THE SEA

Tiny drops on a wet hand
is the clearest image
of the memory of you.
The emotions
and the taste you leave on the skin
are unique in the world.
My heart
goes crazy when you look at me
and every beat of my heart
is an explosion of joy
to see such beauty.
But bitter tears
Slide down my cheeks
leaving strange lines on my skin
which seem to dig deeper
into my sadness
when I leave you.
You are wonderful in my eyes
and in the eyes of many
and I belong to you.
I belong to you
now and forever.

LORD OF THE WAVES

Sweet summer poetry
in this star-filled night
where the total darkness speaks of you.
Where it's wonderful to dream
every distant sunset
and every overseas landscape
I'd like to see with you.
And yet I'm here, far away,
my heart,
my emotions
search for you.
And this desire that surges
makes me think of you among the billowing
waves,
at each tide I seek you with my thoughts,
with my gaze.
And in my heart,
in my memories
while the waves rage
and the lightning flashes,
in the perfect storm where nobody dares,
your sail alone battles wildly
to draw perfect lines
in that sea forgotten by God.
But you are much more than this,

you are unique
and only when the board
seems to have tamed
the fury around it,
your heart is appeased
and you come ashore, no more.
On your smiling face
there's just the sign of the sea
how to forget it
yet in my heart
there's only you, oh my lord.
My lord of the waves.

PLACE OF MY DESIRES

Beyond the white dunes
where the sea
begins its sprawl,
I feel the warm salty breeze
pervade my senses
while my gaze
is lost on the horizon.
The sky
is bluer
than I've ever seen it
and the foamy water on the shore
is brilliant green.
Tongues of sand
alternate in strange geometrical designs,
while the sea
and its waves
never want to let go.
Worn-out shells on the shore
mark time
and the taste of salt
remains forever.
Nights,
deepest black,
kissed by the cosmos
and its creations,

paint a strange canvas
above my head
and in my imagination
I reach out my hand
to scrape a piece away.
And in all this my heart is lost.
Living sunny days
in absolute happiness
and calm nights
filled with stars.
In my heart I think always of you.
Place of my desires.

AT THE EDGES OF THE WORLD

How the sea foams
in stormy raging waves.
The evening
came gradually down
over my head
and the wind,
in powerful gusts,
drags madly
at the flag of the sail.
I look around me.
The taut lines are vibrating
and the other sails
are visibly trembling.
The world seems to tell me to run away
from that godforsaken place.
But the call of the sea
that seems even blacker in the darkness,
keeps me here,
at the mercy of its currents
and takes me out
where I love to be.
Where there's no storm
that I don't feel at home in.

BEYOND THE SEA

Sometimes,
my friend,
I lose myself
gazing at the horizon.
The memory of you
never leaves me
and the taste of salt
is always in my mouth, you know?
How I miss you.
I know,
each time we're together
for just a few minutes
but I often seek you
with my gaze,
and even in my dreams.
Soon,
I promise you,
the moment will come,
the season will start
and the days will be finer.
I'll come to you and the blue,
beyond the sea,
beyond dreams,
I'll see you born.
The sky will brush your back

and with your impetuous nature
and the aid of the currents,
I'll watch you grow and arrive
and you and I,
at last,
will be together in our game
made of action,
devotion
and pieces of heart.

REEF

You
who are born of rock
and skeletal shells
and hard coral
make you grow.
You
who can mutate
into surf
or splendid atoll.
Time
is on your side.
The seasons
see you grow
and change.
The tides caress you
with their gentle touch
and the sun,
with its long rays
penetrates the water
and gives you beautiful highlights.
You
who are always the most
lovely around a volcano
and after
every eruption,

every magma life cycle,
only you remain
in a glorious
ring of nature.

STORMY WAVE

You engulf all you meet
growing great
among so many others.
And when you reach
the height of your power
you make yourself known.
You smash yourself on the cliffs
but unyielding
you continue to the shore.
And only then
you spill over
to die happy on dry land.

LEGEND OF THE SEA

Legend
you dazzle me from the sea
and the heat
of the sun
kisses your
perfect profile.
Legend
in the deep
your face is hidden
among white foam
and stormy billows.
Legend
you play with the sail,
from one wave to the next,
in colourful movement
that from a distance
blinds my avid gaze.
Where gusts of wind
ruffle your hair
and where rays of sun
caress your polished
amber skin,
making my heart leap
every time I see you jump.
Legend

from the heart of the sea
and in my heart
forever
I'll see you happy among the waves.

BATHED IN SALT

Soothed
by the calm
of an autumn dawn
I watch the sea.
And from the tepid warmth
of this sun
hidden in the mist
I observe the waves
breaking on the shore.
Everything's extinguished.
The days,
the happiness.
I close my eyes a moment
and my heart
calls to you.
But from the sea
no sail comes.
Then
my gaze lowers, disappointed.
And waits,
lifeless,
in a sigh
of tired
emotions.
It waits for spring

and your arrival
with your sail
and your appetite for life
to fill my heart
again
with so much joy
how lovely
is the smile
your serene lips
place on your face
bathed in salt.

AND YOU'LL LOVE IT FOREVER

You know the sea
in all its beauty.
You know the world
concealed beneath it.
You live a unique sensation
listening to the silence
of this paradise
and its life forms.
Try it.
And you'll love it forever.

AND I WAIT

How you foam, sea
when I feel the call.
I go into the water
and I see you grow.
You rise
beneath me
and it's like moving
lightly.
Then
I slide down
from your crest
and await your fall.
And I wait.
I wait for you to catch me
in this game of ours
and the higher you rise
the steeper you become.
And I
descend fast
cutting your surface,
defying the current
and then I turn
and take you sideways.
I play with your crest
where it grows white

*as you fold over on yourself
little by little.
But I
follow you fearlessly.
You're beautiful.
And in the tunnel of emotions
on the other side
is the most wonderful view.*

UNEXPECTED CALL

I thank you,
noble-soul man.
I thank you
for letting me remember
how I love the sea.
What I love the most in the world
is not myself
but something much bigger.
A world
as yet undiscovered
which stole my heart
a lifetime ago.
You're a truly special person
to have understood
to have understood me
and so
I think of you
and I imagine you at the edge of the sea
and it seems
so beautiful.
You and it.
Then I think about when you come back to
me
and I'll examine your eyes
in the hope

of seeing something magical
and I'll see something
that I've never seen
before.
And like tiny fireflies
your eyes
will light up at my gaze,
a smile and a few words
whispered
on the breath of the wind...
I MISS YOU.
And I'll never know
if it's your heart
I hear
or the echo of the sea.

YOU ARE SEA

The colour of your eyes.
The depth of your gaze.
You are sea.
The submerged world
you'd like to inhabit.
The wave
that takes me to shore
after the most glorious adventure.
You are sea.
The expanse of water
where I can seek
all my dreams.
The line of the horizon
where everything ends.
You're there.

STORM SURGE

Storm surge
that brings ashore
everything
your rage tore away.
It's a cold wind
that comes with
these freezing waters
of abandonment.
A shell
on the water's edge
moves slightly,
dragged
by the undulations of your reflection
on the sand.
Silence has fallen
and only
the end remains.
The end
of a broken life
at the mercy
of a sea current
that will never end.

INDELIBLE MEMORY

With my nose in the air
I watch the sky.
It's turned red
and this seaside sunset
is a hurricane of emotions.
The waves
rise
and the emotion overflows.
A sail
on the horizon
is like an exquisite painting.
An implacable love.
An indelible memory.

RIDING THE WAVE

I will ride you
boldly
brushing the sky with my fingertips
and when the white foam
falls from your crest,
under you,
I'll brush past your side
and in the tunnel of emotions
I'll come out happy
with you chasing me
and in an overwhelming game of emotions
you'll smile at me happily.

LOVING LOOK

Love,
you come from the sea
with the song of the wind
and from the back of a wave
you smile at me.
Love,
whose gaze is lost
between the blue of the sky
and the deep blue waves.
Love,
whose dream is lost
among foamy crests
and my loving look.
Love,
from the blue of the sea
and the sky blue of your eyes
I am lost.
I dream.
I love.

THE BIGGEST ONE

You were born on the horizon.
From the horizon you come
with distance making you grow
and the force of the tide.
You rise towards the sky
in all your majesty
seeking your glory
to continue with all your fury
and power to the world.

GIFT FROM OVERSEAS

Abandoned shells on the sand
by the water's edge
signal a memory.
A gift brought from far away
and a heartfelt thought
that has crossed the ocean
and flown to me.

FANTASTIC LOVE

Unspoilt purity
that engraves memories on the heart
and with secret voices
ruffles the sea.

TRUTH

A precious jewel.
A unique love.
An ideal that blooms.
A wave forged
by the enchantment of the tides.
A secret
guarded forever
in the blue depths
of this loving heart of mine.

SECRETS

Behind your hard gaze
gusts of wind are hidden.
While behind your beautiful smile
there's love for a wave.
The perfect wave.
I,
my friend,
have you hidden in my heart
and your love for the sea.

EVERLASTING LOVE

You are water.
Everlasting love.
An ocean of complex emotions
that make my life irreplaceable.

THE COAST OF DREAMS

Stormy wave
you arrive from the sea,
blunted by the coast,
along the coast of dreams
that this loving heart of mine
now and forever
will follow you with its gaze.

HIDDEN DESIRE

You're like a storm
that destroys.
An ocean of fire
that burns inside
every emotion.
You what's lost
when a breath of wind passes
across the tight embrace
of a loving look.

BLADE
BLADE 5.3

MY BLUE WORLD

From my window,
open a crack,
a ray of sun
reminds me
how beautiful you are.
There is no equal
to your beauty
and your depths
shroud my curiosity in mystery.
I'll never be tired
of looking at you,
I'll never be tired
of touching you.
It's as if every single part of you
belonged to me
and every part of my body,
including my soul,
is yours.
Sometimes,
I find myself remembering you
in the hottest summer,
when the only breeze
comes from your heart
and its scent
makes me understand

how great you are
and how great
all that belongs to you.
Then I realise
I'm only
a small part of your world,
an insignificant being compared to you,
a tiny part of the cosmos
but one that gives you
your greatest gift.
ETERNAL LOVE.

KNIGHT OF THE SEA

Knight
without armour
your face
is sprinkled with salty drops
that sparkle
in the sun.
You smile.
Games with the sail
turn into incredible emotions
and your lips
rejoice
with every leap on the water.
The sea gets choppy.
The sail turns
and your direction changes.
Before
I could see your gorgeous smile
coming towards me.
Now
your wide shoulders
move away towards the horizon.
Are you leaving, Knight of the Sea?
My eyes follow you.
My heart loves you.

LOVE FROM THE SEA

It's a windy day.
The sun is high.
The sea is beautiful
like never before.
A series of hills and valleys
made of waves
accompanied by
gusts of wind.
White foam
combines with sea-blue
to paint this scene I love so much.
A plunge
into the blue of this ocean.
This paradise
I never tire of.
I surface.
And suddenly a shadow
blocks my sun for an instant.
A sail
passes fast
over the surface of the water
and your smile
meets my eyes.
The most beautiful smile
I've ever seen.

TO BE

You conceal the depth of your gaze
behind black sunglasses
and the security
of bronzed flesh.
The idea of a myth.
A legend
that never fades.
Perseverance
in the search for a wave
that will never cease to be.

WITHOUT YOU I CANNOT STAY

Sea
that takes my memories far away,
my thoughts.
Drowns all my dreams.
My desires.
Sea
without you I cannot stay..
I cannot live.
Sea
you are my world.
My life.

INDEX

LIFE 8

MY WORLD 10

MY LOVE FOR THE SEA 12

LORD OF THE WAVES 14

PLACE OF MY DESIRES 16

AT THE EDGES OF THE WORLD 18

BEYOND THE SEA 20

REEF 22

STORMY WAVE 24

LEGEND OF THE SEA 26

AND YOU'LL LOVE IT FOREVER 30

AND I WAIT 32

UNEXPECTED CALL 34

YOU ARE SEA 36

STORM SURGE 38

INDELIBLE MEMORY 39

RIDING THE WAVE...40

LOVING LOOK...42

THE BIGGEST ONE...43

GIFT FROM OVERSEAS 44

FANTASTIC LOVE..46

TRUTH..47

SECRETS..48

EVERLASTING LOVE..50

THE COAST OF DREAMS.......................................51

HIDDEN DESIRE..52

MY BLUE WORLD 54

KNIGHT OF THE SEA...56

LOVE FROM THE SEA 58

TO BE..59

WITHOUT YOU I CANNOT STAY............................60

ACKNOWLEDGEMENTS

A love for the sea, sprung from the wind and its strong currents and the constant quest for the perfect wave, led me to admire this man whose purity made me a part of his world, albeit for a short time, transmitting to me this love whose simplicity bewitched my heart and inspired some of the best poems I have ever written. Heartfelt thanks.

Printed in the month of November 2015
on behalf of Youcanprint Self-Publishing

9 788889 321276 2